SKYLARK CHOOSE YOUR OWN ADVENTURE® • 7

"I DON'T LIKE CHOOSE YOUR OWN ADVENTURE® BOOKS. I *LOVE* THEM!" says Jessica Gordon, age 10. And now, kids between the ages of six and nine can choose their own adventure, too. Here's what kids have to say about the new Skylark Choose Your Own Adventure® books.

"These are my favorite books because you can pick whatever choice you want— and the story is all about you."
—**Katy Alson,** *age 8*

"I love finding out how my story will end."
—**Joss Williams,** *age 9*

"I like all the illustrations!"
—**Savitri Brightfield,** *age 7*

"A six-year-old friend and I have lots of fun making the decisions together."
—**Peggy Marcus** *(adult)*

Bantam Skylark Books in the Choose Your Own
  Adventure® Series
Ask your bookseller for the books you have missed

# HELP! YOU'RE SHRINKING

## EDWARD PACKARD

# ILLUSTRATED BY LORNA TOMEI

A BANTAM SKYLARK BOOK®
TORONTO · NEW YORK · LONDON · SYDNEY

RL 2, 007-009

HELP! YOU'RE SHRINKING

*A Bantam Skylark Book / April 1983*

CHOOSE YOUR OWN ADVENTURE® *is a registered trademark of Bantam Books, Inc.*

*Original conception of Edward Packard*

*Skylark Books is a registered trademark of Bantam Books, Inc. Registered in U.S. Patent and Trademark Office and elsewhere.*

*Cover art by Paul Granger*

ISBN 0-553-15195-9

*Published simultaneously in the United States and Canada*

---

Bantam Books are published by Bantam Books, Inc. Its trademark, consisting of the words "Bantam Books" and the portrayal of a rooster, is Registered in U.S. Patent and Trademark Office and in other countries. Marca Registrada. Bantam Books, Inc., 666 Fifth Avenue, New York, New York 10103.

---

PRINTED IN THE UNITED STATES OF AMERICA

CW     0 9 8 7 6 5 4 3 2 1

To those who would rather be taller
or shorter
or thinner
or fatter
and to those who would not

## READ THIS FIRST!!!

Most books are about other people.

This book is about you—and your dog, Dusty.

*What happens to you depends on what you decide to do.*

Do not read this book from the first page through to the last page. Instead, start on page one and read until you come to your first choice. Then turn to the page shown and see what happens.

When you come to the end of a story, go back and start again. Every choice leads to a new adventure.

Be careful! If you don't watch out, you might start to shrink. Then who knows what will happen?

You and Dusty are walking through the tall **1**
marsh grass along the edge of Duck Pond.
Dusty is big, shaggy, and black. He's the best
dog you've ever had. The two of you are
looking for turtles, but what catches your eye
is a large bottle leaning against a log. There's
a label on it:

> DANGER: DO NOT TOUCH
>
> RETURN TO PROFESSOR RIGA
>
> 14 DUCK POND ROAD

There's no cap on the bottle, which is half
filled with blue liquid.

---

*If you decide to pick up the bottle,*
*turn to page 2.*

*If you decide not to pick up the bottle,*
*turn to page 4.*

**2**    You pick up the bottle. It's slippery and you lose your grip on it. Some liquid splashes on your arm as the bottle falls to the ground.

You'd better wash this stuff off in the pond. You start toward the pond, but you trip on the log. It seems bigger than before. What's more, the grass seems to be growing right in front of your eyes. And the trees around you are climbing toward the sky.

*Help, you're shrinking!*

*If you try to wash your arm in the pond, turn to page 6.*

*If you run home to get help, turn to page 22.*

**4**  You decide not to pick up the bottle.

"Let's look over this way," you say to Dusty.

But Dusty is sniffing the bottle. He looks at you curiously and bounds off into the woods.

Where has that dog gone? Probably chasing a rabbit. You poke around in the brush. Suddenly, a small black dog runs right at you. It jumps against your legs as if it knows you. Good grief, it's Dusty, only much smaller! The poor dog is shrinking before your eyes! You glance toward the bottle. It has tipped over. Some of the liquid has spilled out.

You've got to get Dusty to a vet. You start to pick him up, but then you stop. If you touch him, will you start shrinking too?

*If you run home to get help for Dusty, turn to page 11.*

*If you pick up Dusty and carry him home, turn to page 12.*

*If you pick up both Dusty and the bottle, turn to page 14.*

You want to wash off your arm. The pond is only a few feet away, but it seems much farther. You have trouble getting through the giant blades of grass. By now you're only a few inches tall.

Blocking your way to the pond is a huge animal, big as a wolf, with a mouth twice as

large, and a horrible green face and bulging eyes. It's a frog.

SNAP! The frog's long tongue darts out at you. You leap out of the way just in time.

*Go on to page 8.*

**8**    BZZZZZ. To your left, yellow and black helicopters fly over giant daisies. But they're not helicopters—they're hornets. BZZZZZ. Their stingers look like long swords. One sting would finish you off.

You turn to the right. Just as you think you are safely past the frog, you see a creature

with a horrible face and jaws like a monster. **9**
It's only a muskrat, but you've shrunk so fast
that it's bigger than you are.

There's no time to think. You've got to get
to the water fast.

---

*If you try to run past the muskrat,*
*turn to page 16.*

*If you try to duck past the hornets,*
*turn to page 18.*

You run home and tell your mom all about **11** Dusty shrinking.

"I'll believe it when I see it," says Mom, "so let's go have a look."

As the two of you start down the road, a small animal scampers toward you.

"Mom! Look, it's Dusty!"

"Oh, no. It must be a mouse."

You can't blame Mom for not believing her eyes. But *you* know what a mouse looks like, and you know what Dusty looks like.

Suddenly a gray cat sneaks up on you. Quickly you grab your tiny dog away from the cat's sharp claws.

"That was a close call," Mom says, "but what will happen to Dusty when we're not around?"

"We'll have to get a regular-sized dog to guard him," you reply. "Can we, Mom?"

"Yes," she says with a smile, "but only if you'll promise to keep him away from strange-looking bottles!"

**The End**

**12**    You pick up Dusty and run home.

"Where did you get that tiny dog?" your mom asks. "And where's Dusty?"

You start to explain, but you hardly need to. Dusty is still shrinking.

"Oh my gosh!" Mom exclaims. "We've got to get this dog to the vet."

You drop Dusty gently into your shirt pocket and jump into the car. Mom drives lickety-split to the veterinarian's office. As you ride along, you hear little barks coming from your pocket. By the time you arrive, your poor dog has shrunk even more.

*Go on to the next page.*

Dr. Kemp, the vet, peers at Dusty through a magnifying glass. "Good heavens, this is startling!" She hands you an empty cup. "Put Dusty in here so he won't get lost."

You tell Dr. Kemp about the bottle near the pond. "Is there anything you can do?" you ask.

*Turn to page 20.*

**14**     You cradle Dusty in your arms, pick up the bottle, and start for home. Suddenly Dusty leaps from your arms, knocking the bottle out of your hand. Blue liquid spills all over you. Dusty runs into the tall grass. But you don't have time to worry about him. You've started to shrink too!

Your house is a half mile away. Should you try to make it home, or should you run to the nearest house for help?

*If you try to make it home,*
*turn to page 22.*

*If you head for the nearest house,*
*turn to page 26.*

**16** Muskrats look fierce when they're bigger than you are. You run past the muskrat and into the pond, which by now looks like an ocean. You wade in and wash your arm.

Suddenly a big wave hits you, and you struggle to get out. Exhausted, you flop on the ground.

Luckily you've stopped shrinking.

*Turn to page 21.*

**18**    Hornets don't sting everyone who passes by, so maybe they won't sting you. You run quickly, keeping an eye on the hornets so you can duck if one of them flies near you.

*Turn to page 26.*

**20**    Dr. Kemp shakes her head. "I'm afraid there's nothing I can do. I've never seen a case like this."

"The label on the bottle said 'Danger,' and it gave a name and address, but I don't remember them," you say.

"We've got to find that bottle before anyone else touches it," Dr. Kemp says. "If that blue liquid gets into the wrong hands, it could shrink hundreds of people. Will you show me where you found it?"

You want to help, but you don't want to go near that bottle again. You might start to shrink, too.

If you agree to help, turn to page 47.

If you decide not to risk it, turn to page 30.

You start the long walk back home, keep- **21**
ing your eye out for any hawks that might
mistake you for a chipmunk. Judging by the
height of some nearby dandelions, you must
be about three inches tall. At this height,
when you grow up, you might reach five
inches.

What kind of life lies ahead for you? You
could become a midget in the circus. But you
have a better idea. You'll become a scientist
and find the secret formula that will make
you grow.

## The End

**22**   As you run for home, the trees and houses seem to grow larger and larger. But you know that you're just getting smaller.

You scream, but your voice sounds no louder than a kitten's meow. No one will hear you.

You stop to catch your breath. Suddenly a huge, black shape appears. It's an animal as big as a bear. You shriek with fear, but then you realize that it's Dusty. Even though Dusty has shrunk, he's not nearly as small as you are.

It would take forever to get home. Maybe you could ride on Dusty's back. But there's a problem. Dusty loves to roll over in the grass, and he might roll right over you.

*If you climb onto Dusty's back,
turn to page 32.*

*If you keep running toward home,
turn to page 34.*

**24**    "Come in," you say to Professor Riga. "Do you really think you can get Dusty back to his right size?"

The professor's eyes blink rapidly. "Yes, that's why I've come. I was afraid something like this might happen," he says. "Luckily I have been able to invent an antidote. It's a green liquid that will make Dusty grow."

You put Dusty on the floor, and the professor takes a bottle from his pocket. You watch anxiously. How can the professor be sure of pouring the right amount?

"Is this dangerous?" you ask. The professor looks at you and blinks again. "Well, it's a little risky, I suppose. I've never tried it before."

---

*If you let the professor pour the antidote on Dusty, turn to page 29.*

*If you tell him not to risk it, turn to page 48.*

**26** You want to get to the nearest house for help. You're still shrinking. Your right leg slips into a mousehole, and you fall flat on your face!

You try to get up, but you can't. Instead you fall deeper into the mousehole. The sides are too steep for you to climb.

Looking around the hole, you see that it leads to an enormous cave. What would you do if a mouse came out?

You're shrinking so fast the mouse probably wouldn't even notice you, for by now you are no larger than an ant. You're sure of that because an ant is heading toward you. It looks about four feet long. You hide behind a pebble.

What used to be a tiny puddle of water in **27** the mousehole is now, to you, a large pond. Should you jump in?

---

*If you jump into the pond, turn to page 40.*

*If you stay where you are, turn to page 44.*

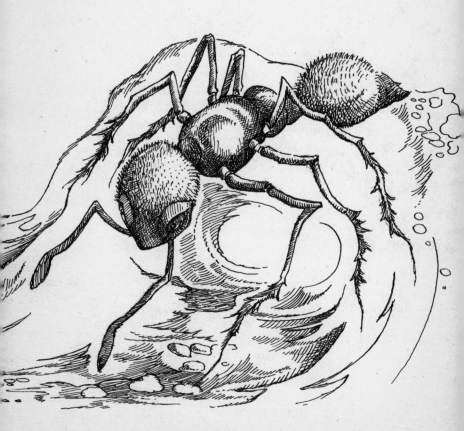

The professor pours the green liquid on
Dusty.

"Oh, no! What have I done?" the professor cries as Dusty starts to grow. In seconds he is as tall as the dining room table, and still growing.

"Can't you do something?" you shout. "Dusty is turning into a monster!"

But the professor only yells back, "No, no, I am the monster for inventing such a thing!" And he runs out the door.

Dusty rests a paw on your shoulder. He's trying to be friendly, but he almost knocks you to the floor.

You reach up and pat Dusty's chest. "Lie down, boy."

Dusty curls up on the floor. He stretches halfway across the room! At last he stops growing.

You are now the owner of the biggest dog in the world.

**The End**

**30**    "Sorry, I don't want to get near that stuff again," you tell Dr. Kemp.

Later that day, when you are back at home, you hear a knock on the door. You open it and find a man standing there. He has thick white hair and blue eyes that blink rapidly.

"I'm Professor Riga, the inventor," the man says. "Someone saw you walking near Duck Pond this morning. Did you happen to see a bottle with blue fluid in it?"

"*See* it? It shrank my dog!"

Tears well up in the professor's eyes. "I feel terrible. It was so careless of me to drop that bottle. Please let me come in. I want to try to get your dog back to the right size."

*Turn to page 24.*

**32**　You climb onto Dusty's back. "Quick! Home, boy, home!" you shout.

Dusty starts running, while you grab on to his fur. But you're still shrinking. Soon you're so tiny that a single strand of dog hair feels like a thick rope. As you shrink, the rope feels like a tree trunk. Soon it's too thick for you to grip. *Help, you're falling*—into a puddle of water that looks like a big pond.

Good luck!

## The End

You keep running toward home, but you're still shrinking. The smaller you get, the less ground you cover. It takes you almost a minute to run past a parked car!

SPLASH. A bucket of water lands on your head. SPLASH, SPLASH, SPLASH. You look up. Suddenly you realize that the buckets of water are only raindrops. Then you see what looks like a long glass building. When

you get closer, you can tell that it's only an empty soda bottle. You crawl into it to get out of the rain. The moment you're inside, you're swept up high into the air. Rolling wildly around, you realize that someone has picked up the bottle with you inside.

*Go on to page 36.*

**36**     From inside the soda bottle, you see a man with white hair. "Oh, dear, I was afraid this would happen," he says. "I'm Professor Riga. I'm sorry you shrank, but don't worry. I can make you grow again!"

You yell at the professor, trying to get him to hold the bottle steady, but he can't hear your tiny voice.

He enters a house and sets the soda bottle down on the floor. "Now stay in the bottle," he tells you. "I'll be right back."

Can you trust the professor? Maybe you should try to get away.

---

*If you wait for the professor to come back, turn to page 38.*

*If you crawl out of the bottle and try to escape, turn to page 52.*

**38**     You wait in the bottle, shivering. You're wet from the rain and sticky from the leftover soda in the bottle.

The professor has returned. "Aha! It was here all the time." He picks up a bottle of green liquid from the table. "This is a growing potion. It will make you grow as fast as you shrank. I think it would be best if we went outside where you'll have plenty of room."

*Go on to the next page.*

The professor carries the bottle outside and shakes you onto the grass. Nearby a robin, looking as big as an ostrich, is hunting for worms. You'd like to climb on its back and take a ride.

*If you climb onto the robin's back, turn to page 50.*

*If you ask the professor to give you the growing potion, turn to page 42.*

**40**     You jump into the pond and land on a floating leaf. The wind begins to blow you across the pond.

By the time you reach the other side, you've shrunk even more. You climb off the leaf and onto shore.

You see another monster nearby. This time it's a grasshopper. Since you could use a ride, you jump on its back.

POING! The grasshopper hops. POING! It hops again. You hang on for your life!

POING! The biggest hop of all sends you flying through an open kitchen window.

*Go on to the next page.*

PLOP! You land in a bowl of chocolate pudding. Mmmmmm. It's delicious. Mmmm. It's the best you've ever tasted. Soon you're full of chocolate pudding, and you're having trouble swimming. The sides of the bowl are too steep to climb out.

SLURP, SLURP, GLURP!

*Help, you're sinking!*

## The End

**42**   "I'd like to get back to my own size *right now*," you shout.

The professor takes a deep breath and then pours a bottle of green liquid over your head. Instantly you start growing. But something is wrong. You're growing too fast. In a few seconds, you're as tall as the professor.

"*Stop me!*" you yell. You look down but you can barely see your feet.

A small voice calls up to you from below, "Sorry. I poured on too much."

Soon you have grown higher than the rooftops. You shout at the top of your lungs, "*Help, I'm growing!*"

## The End

**44**    As you stand in the mousehole, you continue to shrink. The ant looks like a giant, and you feel as if you are standing in a field surrounded by mountains.

Suddenly, tiny creatures are all around you. Perhaps they are bacteria. Even these tiny creatures grow larger and larger before your eyes.

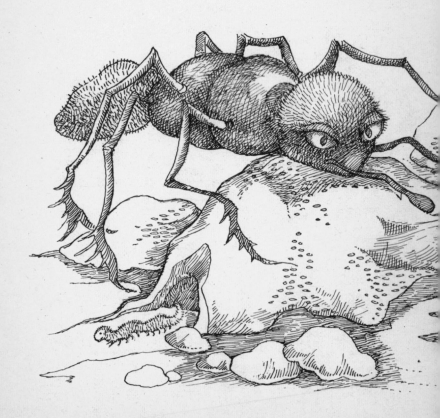

You continue to shrink. Soon you're **45** smaller than a speck of dust. Now no one can see you without a microscope.

What will happen to you? How much smaller can you get? How small, you wonder, can *anything* be?

**The End**

"I'll help you find the bottle," you say to
Dr. Kemp.

When you and Dr. Kemp reach the pond, you see a short, white-haired man holding a bottle. "Have you seen a bottle filled with blue liquid?" he calls. "I've lost my shrinking fluid."

"So you're the one!" you exclaim.

"Yes. I'm Professor Riga, the inventor. I made two bottles of shrinking fluid. I left one near here by mistake. I hope nobody shrank."

"My dog shrank," you tell him.

Suddenly Professor Riga spots the blue bottle behind a log. He picks it up and without another word pours the contents of one bottle into the other. A cloud of steam rises in the air.

"What did you do?" asks Dr. Kemp.

The professor blinks his eyes. "I shrank the shrinking fluid," he says with relief.

"Great," you say. "But what about my dog?"

**The End**

**48**   "I don't want you to use that stuff on Dusty," you say.

The professor blinks his eyes. "Goodbye, then," he says. "I'll never trouble you again."

You and your family are upset, but Dusty seems as happy as ever. He has a lot more room to run around. And, of course, it costs a lot less to feed him.

People come from all over to see your dog. They can hardly believe he's real.

No one ever sees Professor Riga again. His house is empty. Some people say that he accidentally spilled his formula on himself and shrank completely away.

## The End

**50** You leap onto the robin's back and hang on for your life as it soars up past the tree-tops. WHOOSH. The robin shakes you off into a nest with three baby robins. SQUAWK. SQUAWK. Their mouths are wide open as they stretch toward the mother bird. She dangles a fat worm above you. She must think you're a baby robin! The worm lands on your head. A baby robin gobbles it up. The mother robin flies off.

You look over the edge of the nest. "HELP!" you yell as loudly as you can.

How can you get down? You look around the nest. Among the twigs is some string and a piece of cloth.

"This is no life for me," you tell the baby robins. "I'm going to make a parachute and get out of here."

## The End

**52**   You crawl out of the soda bottle. You see another bottle nearby, filled with green liquid. On it is a label that says "ANTIDOTE."

Antidote! That's just what you need to get back to your right size. You pour some on yourself. Instantly you start to grow.

Soon you find yourself back to normal size. Dusty is licking your ear, probably wondering why you've been sleeping all afternoon. You realize that you and Dusty never did shrink at all. The bottle you picked up must have contained a *sleeping* potion, not a shrinking potion!

"Come on, Dusty," you say as you get to your feet. "We'll be late for dinner."

## The End

## ABOUT THE AUTHOR

**Edward Packard,** a graduate of Princeton University and Columbia Law School, practiced law in New York and Connecticut before turning to writing full time. He developed the unique storytelling approach used in the CHOOSE YOUR OWN ADVENTURE® series while thinking up stories for his children, Caroline, Andrea, and Wells.

## ABOUT THE ILLUSTRATOR

**Lorna Tomei** studied painting and illustration at the Art Students League and the School of Visual Arts in New York. She has illustrated more than a dozen children's books and is a frequent contributor to children's magazines. Ms. Tomei lives in Centerport, Long Island with her husband, two sons, one dog, three rats, two cats, and a very crabby parrot.

# WANT TO READ THE MOST EXCITING BOOKS AROUND?
# CHOOSE CHOOSE YOUR OWN ADVENTURE®

Everybody loves CHOOSE YOUR OWN ADVENTURE® books because the stories are about *you*. Each book is loaded with choices that only *you* can make. Instead of reading from the first page to the last page, you read until you come to your first choice. Then, depending on your decision, you turn to a new page to see what happens next. And you can keep reading and rereading CHOOSE YOUR OWN ADVENTURE® books because every choice leads to a new adventure and there are lots of different ways for the story to end.

Buy these great CHOOSE YOUR OWN ADVENTURE® books, available wherever Bantam Skylark books are sold or use the handy coupon below for ordering: